The Proud Hippo

by June Woodman
Illustrated by Ken Morton

Hippo looks at herself in the still water of her pool. She is proud of her dainty feet. She is very proud of the new hat she has made for the Safari Supper. It is piled high with cherries, plums, grapes and bananas. It has an orange and some vine leaves on it too.
"How beautiful I look," sighs Hippo.

She goes to see Alligator.
He is on his muddy bank.
"Look how beautiful I am
in my new hat," cries Hippo,
running down to show him.
Her feet get muddy, but
Hippo is too big to see them.
"Fruit!" yells Alligator.
"Just what we want for . . .
oops!" He slips on the mud
and splashes Hippo,
but she doesn't notice.

Hippo goes to see Elephant
in his orange grove.
"Look how beautiful I am
in my new hat," she calls.
"Huh!" says Elephant. "You
don't look very beautiful
to me. And that's my orange!"
Elephant grabs it, but Hippo
doesn't notice.

As Hippo goes down the path, leaves and grass stick to her muddy feet. They do not look very dainty now, but Hippo is too big to see. She can see Monkey, though. He is up in a tree.

Monkey is hanging upside down
by his tail.
"Look how beautiful I am
in my new hat," calls Hippo.
"Turn around," says Monkey
with a wicked grin.
Hippo gives a dainty twirl.
She does not see Monkey grab
the bananas from her hat.

Hippo goes on – clump, clump.
"It's hot in the sun,"
she puffs. She sits down
under a tree to rest.
Ostrich is picking plums
from the same tree.
She picks the plums on Hippo's
hat by mistake.
"Oooh-er, sorry," whispers
Ostrich and she turns
bright red.

Ostrich hides her head
in her bucket.
"Now you can't see how
beautiful I am in my new hat,"
says Hippo. "Anyway, your
bucket isn't nearly as fine
as my hat."
Hippo goes on her way,
with her nose in the air.

Hippo clumps on. She meets
Kangaroo teaching Baby
how to count with cherries.
Hippo sits down beside them.
"Look how beautiful I am
in my new hat," she says.
"Oh yes," says Kangaroo.
Then she starts to count,
"One, two, three!"
"Four, five, six!" shouts Baby,
picking the cherries from
Hippo's hat. But Hippo
doesn't notice.

Hippo plods on to see Giraffe.
He is cooking vine leaf soup.
"Look how beautiful I am
in my new hat," calls Hippo.
Giraffe looks down on her.
"Too many vine leaves, I think,"
says Giraffe. "Let me help."
Giraffe takes the vine leaves
from her hat and drops them
in the soup pot.

Hippo goes on with only grapes left on her hat. Parrot comes swooping down.

"Grapes! Grapes!" she squawks.

"Yes, my hat is great, isn't it?" smiles Hippo proudly.

Parrot swoops away. She says nothing at all. Her beak is too full of Hippo's grapes.

Soon the Safari Supper is ready. Each animal brings something to eat. First they have Giraffe's vine leaf soup. Then they eat Kangaroo's fruit salad. Ostrich has made plum pudding. Monkey serves banana splits. They all go on to Hippo's pool for drinks.

When she arrives at her pool, Hippo looks at herself in the water. Her hat is quite bare and she is covered in mud from her head to her feet. "My beautiful hat!" cries Hippo. "Oh I look such a mess," she wails.

Baby Kangaroo runs over
to hug Hippo.
"We love you for what you are,
not for how you look," he says.
And that is something to make
anyone proud.

Here are some words in the story.

dainty	count
beautiful	many
notice	sneers
though	plods
wicked	swooping
twirl	bare
clump	wails